I0624657

Parallel Encounters

Salvage

Book 2

David Scott Fields II

Anchorage, Alaska
www.thrivechristianpress.com

Thrive Christian Press
1120 Huffman Rd. Ste. 24-447
Anchorage, AK 99515

First published by Thrive Christian Press on December 25,
2014.

ISBN 978-0-692-35235-9

Published in the United States of America.

This book is dedicated to Justin and Lynsey Hostetter, true friends and servants of Christ. Long may you serve Him in faithfulness and truth!

Reader's Note

This novella continues the story begun in *Parallel Encounters – The Prism's Echo*. Four years have passed, and with the rebels now in control of the Space Port, the tides of the war with Saki Chu and his New Nazi Confederation have changed for the better. However, some good things were never meant to last.

Before

"I know what you're thinking."

"Huh? What?" Scotty Fields, the young emperor of Staranana, jumped and looked up from the table he was sitting at to see the petite and lovely (for a bear) chief physician of Staranana, Dr. Gloria Moonbeam.

"Spikey and Sparkey told me about the *Prism's Echo* and what happened to both you and Spikey. You've hardly left this library since then, and that was a week ago."

"I'm sorry, Gloria. I know I've been a little antisocial lately."

Gloria slipped into a chair beside him, tapped his hand gently and said, "It's all right. Things have been pretty quiet around here since we got back. Garlan and TB are still off at the cave church analyzing all the data we collected in the biblical past. Chef Berry has locked himself in his kitchen getting ready for Thanksgiving. Spikey and Nicodemus are off analyzing the *Prism's Echo*, and everyone else seems to be making themselves scarce as well. I haven't treated anything worse than a paper cut since we got back."

"Well, with the holidays just around the corner, I imagine it won't stay that way for long. Is Chef Berry upset that I want him to prepare the Palace for yet another human holiday tradition?"

Gloria chuckled as she answered, "Ha! You know Chef. He always finds things to complain about, but cooking is what he loves, and from what you've described, Thanksgiving sounds like the ultimate feast."

"Yeah, I guess so."

"But I am assuming our chef's disposition isn't what has you hiding in this library."

"No, I guess not. I've just been thinking, and this is a good place to do it."

"Have you been thinking about what happened in the past? Do you really think the Viper is…"

"Oh, no, it's nothing to do with that. I will admit that I am a bit jealous that you all got to see Christ resurrect, but it's not like I was wanting for the miraculous on that journey. Actually, I was thinking about my friends in the parallel universe."

"Scotty, that was just a fantasy."

"What if it wasn't? What if there really is a reality out there where I'm an orphan and all humanity is under the control of a Nazi regime a thousand times worse than the original one under Hitler?"

"I'd say that is about as likely as our world being nothing more than the product of some man sitting at a keyboard typing away right now."

Scotty's face twisted into a frown. "That's not funny, Gloria!"

"Sorry, but it's not as if you can go back, at least not until we learn more about the *Prism's Echo* and how to keep from getting lost in it."

"You're right, but it's not like I need the book. My own imagination is going wild with possibilities."

"Good or bad?"

"A little of both. I left just before they would have captured the Space Port."

"You think they made it don't you?"

"Their plan was a good one, but then again, King Arthur was mortally wounded by Mordred in that legend. Spikey left Camelot before that could happen, but that doesn't mean it won't still happen."

"Oh, brother! Okay, so what do you suggest?"

"I don't know, but I have about a dozen possible scenarios spinning around in my head."

"And how do they go?"

"Well, the best and admittedly the most likely scenario has the rebels seizing the Space Port and holding it without incident for about four years."

"Four years! Where did you get that number?"

"I remember Agent Loso saying the station could go for about four years without recharging its energy reserves. If the rebels had an overabundance of energy reserves, I doubt they would be on the defensive so much. After four years, Captain Brooks (and yes I would give her a promotion if *Rebel Command* hasn't already) and her crew will be forced to start searching for more power. Plus, there is also the fact that in four years my duplicate will be 15, and 15 is way cooler than 11."

"I see, and do the rebels succeed in their quest?"

"That's where things start getting interesting. I see it happening like this…"

Chapter 1
The Light Speed Drive

Captain Lori Brooks hesitated before finally rolling to the other side of her bed. After years of sleeping in bedding tubes on the *Intruder*, sleeping on her king size bed on the station had never ceased to feel like a luxury, even after four years. Even so, the comfort of her bed and her quarters - that were literally the size of a small house - notwithstanding, there had never once been a time where she had slept straight through the night since taking the station. Most evenings, she lay awake for hours as a million worries spun through her head. The most prominent one being, *'Where were the Nazis?'*

Four years earlier, the rebels had captured the Space Port without a single casualty on either side. It had taken weeks to bring the station back online. During all that time, the planetary barrier had remained deactivated, and had he wanted to, Emperor Saki Chu could have launched a counterattack with almost guaranteed success.

But he never did. In fact, the few Nazi vessels that remained in the solar system had retreated to the outer rim near Pluto, and they hadn't been heard from since.

When the station was finally back online, everyone assumed the war was over – at least on the space front. *Rebel Command* still wrestled with the question of what to do about those still trapped on Earth, but for the rest of the solar system, there hadn't been so much as a single space battle for years.

Brooks knew that had to change soon enough. In only a matter of months, the station would run out of power, and if Chu didn't launch a counterstrike then, he was an idiot. Yes, it was only a matter of time.

"Captain Brooks, please report to the Command Deck immediately!"

Was this it? Brooks was in the habit of asking herself that question anytime someone summoned her frantically – which, regardless of the four year peace, still seemed to happen quite a bit. It took a second to recognize the deep voice that cried out to her. It was Lieutenant Scott Fields. After four years, he was no longer a boy by any means, and he was rapidly closing in on manhood. His voice had deepened, he had grown about a foot, and Commander Eli had kept him in the gym so much, he was, to use an old slang term, *ripped*.

~

"Oh, yeah, like that's realistic!"

"Hey, Gloria! Who's telling this story – you or me?"

"Sorry! Please, please, continue."

"All right…now where was I? Oh, yes!"

~

"What is it, Lieutenant?"

"Captain, I think the explanation will speak for itself, but you should get up here fast."

~

Moments later, Brooks stepped onto the Command Deck of the Space Port and said, "Let me make one thing clear; I am tired of being told that the explanation will speak for itself. The next time I ask a question, I expect to..." She paused as her eyes landed on the large Nazi holographic display screen, and she asked, "What is that?"

On the display, the holographic counterpart of a saucer shaped vessel burned in space. Eli answered her, "We haven't been able to identify it. It could be a Nazi vessel, but then again, it could be a new Rebel vessel that we haven't been informed of. It's drifting just outside of Mars's orbit."

"Whatever it is, it's sending out a distress call. The signal is very faint. We'd have to get closer to determine exactly what it says, but the energy readings from the ship itself are off the scale," reported Lt. Commander Leah Smith.

Brooks leaned over her tactical officer's console and examined the display. She said, "There seems to be something written on the hull."

"I saw that too, Captain. I can't make out the language, but the station's code breaking software was able to render a word of sorts – *Rimcha.*"

"*Rimcha?*" Brooks repeated. "That's not a human word, is it?"

Smith answered, "Not in any language I have ever studied."

"What, not in any of the 20?" Brooks smirked, well aware of her tactical officer's multilingual background.

Smith returned her captain's grin, but before she could report further, Lt. Fields broke in, "Captain, I am reading a SYCO class vessel moving to intercept the *Rimcha*. It will overtake the vessel in less than fifteen minutes."

"And now it happens," Brooks muttered under her breath. Then to her crew, "Why didn't we detect either vessel before this? Mars is practically next door."

Eli reported, "They both seemed to materialize out of nowhere. I'm guessing Black Vortex technology, Captain."

"Then why did the SYCO ship come out of their jump fifteen minutes from interception with the UFO?"

"It's difficult to speculate, Captain," Smith said. "But given our confused readings, I don't think it's too far of a leap to hypothesize that that vessel is of extraterrestrial origin. The Nazis would love to get their hands on something like that, but they are likely exercising caution."

"Aliens?" Brooks quipped. "Most people stopped evening considering the possibility of extraterrestrial life decades ago. Humanity has been able to send probes out to all the stars within 20 light years since the development of Black Vortex technology. In all that time, not so much as a stray radio signal from an alien civilization has ever been detected. There has to be another explanation."

"That's just what the data seems to indicate, Captain. And regardless of what that ship is, the Nazis are getting closer," Smith reported.

"Well, we're not going to just sit back and watch. If your readings are right, that ship could solve all of our power issues. Commander Eli, what is the status of the *Intruder*?"

"She's in docking bay twenty-three, Captain. I've had a team working to install Nazi weaponry, and I have even had them reinforce the hull with an enhanced titanium armor. The *Intruder* can now take twice the pounding she once could, and she is more ready for combat than ever before. But you're not planning on attacking the aliens, are you, Captain?"

"Whoever they are - I would prefer trying to make some new friends first, but let's be ready for anything. Post a skeleton crew and ready her for launch."

Then Brooks turned to address Chief Josh Austin at the power maintenance grid, "Chief, your analysis? Could we make use of that ship's power?

"I hope so, Captain, but long range sensors can only tell you so much. I would need to get some close range scans."

"Then you're with me. Now we just have to get there. What is the status of the new Light Speed Drive?"

"I've finished the most recent modifications to the unit, and they've been installed. We've come a long way in the last four years, and almost all the trial runs were a success; but this will be the first actual mission we've used it on. I have my doubts about it being 100% successful over a period of extended use."

"Well, Chief, I'm leaving it up to you to see that it does succeed. Report to your station aboard the *Intruder*, and prepare for departure."

After she had said this, she turned to Eli and instructed, "Launch the ship, Commander. Smith and I will take a TSJ over in a few minutes. You and Lt. Fields are to stay here and man the station."

Eli acknowledged his Captain without a second word, but Fields jumped up to protest, "Captain, you can't go out there without me. You need a good helmsman, and I'm still the best one you have."

Brooks was less than impressed with his ego, but she admired his determination. Nonetheless, time was growing short. She said, "Lieutenant, I appreciate your concerns, but I happen to be a capable pilot myself. I will man the helm for now." He tried to protest further, but she silenced him with a glance. Then she and Smith headed off the Command Deck at a run.

~

As Brooks and Smith arrived on the bridge of the *Intruder*, the Captain called out over the intercom, "Chief Austin, are you ready?"

"The drive is online, Captain. I'm recalibrating the gravitational grid to compensate for the inertial stress the drive will produce."

"You mean so we won't get flattened like pancakes? How fast will we be able to go?" she asked.

"No faster than two times light speed, Captain."

"Understood, I'm taking the helm now. Preparing to initiate the drive. I'll engage at your command, Chief."

"Counting   down   from   ten   then.
10…9…8…7…6…5…4…3…2…Now, Captain!"

Brooks pressed her control lever forward, and the ship began to hum with a new energy. The captain would have been hard pressed to describe the situation adequately if she had tried. In one sense, it felt like electric ants were crawling all over her body. In another, it felt like she was immersed in a hot tub of lightning. There was no pain, but every hair on her body was standing on end. This was bound to be a wild ride.

For the most part, Chief Austin, Chief Martinez, and Lt. Fields had conducted the tests on the *Intruder's* new drive. She had only been aboard for the initial test when the ship was brought up to 90% of light speed. It had felt like the ship was going to rip itself apart then, and the gravity generators hadn't been perfectly calibrated at the time, so not only had the lungs of nearly the entire skeleton crew almost collapsed, but everyone's lunch had also been spewed all over the decks. The *Intruder* made its maiden *almost-light speed* voyage to Venus and back with no real casualties, but the entire skeleton crew had been incapacitated for weeks, recovering.

That was almost three years ago, and it hadn't been until the last two years that the project really picked up steam again. The Nazi database and the resources of the station had been invaluable. Brooks had begged off personally supervising any further test flights, but six months earlier, Austin had reported that they had finally broken the LS barrier, and with that obstacle out of the way, they seemed to be adding speed with every passing week.

Now, here she was again, and the sensations were nothing like before. As the semi-electric, tachyon field permeated everyone and everything onboard, inviting them to defy the very laws of physics, the *Intruder* shot forward in space in a rainbow of dazzling color. Brooks watched the holoviewer as starlight bent and twisted and then all but vanished. Outside the ship, every beam of light in the solar system would have been straining to keep up with the *Intruder* – a race they were doomed to lose.

Brooks called out, "Chief, how fast are we going?"

"1.78 times light speed. That's all I can give you, Captain. The drive is already starting to overheat."

"That'll do just fine, Chief. We…" Brooks started, but then the ship bucked and threw her from her seat at the helm. As she staggered back into position, she demanded, "Report!"

"The stress on the hull is extreme, Captain, and one of our reserve thruster fuel tanks just exploded. The gravity generators have been compromised and a massive breech is forming on the belly of the ship. We're being gutted!" Smith exclaimed.

"Transfer all available power to the structural integrity grid!"

"It's no use, Captain! I can't do anything. I've lost my panel!"

Brooks shouted to the intercom above her, "Chief, shut it down!"

"It's too late, Captain! The drive is…"

Chapter 2
The Blue Vortex

"Now this is getting exciting!" Gloria Moonbeam squealed.

"Yeah, but I think if Spikey had been helping Chief Austin, he might have had more success," Scotty said.

"Hey! Credit where credit is due! Even Spikey hasn't gotten his ships up to light speed yet."

"That's true."

"So what happens next? Was the *Intruder* destroyed? Was the crew killed?"

"That wouldn't make much of a story, now would it?"

~

Brooks moved her hand to her forehead as she lay on the cold deck. A bruise the size of a grapefruit was forming, and she had one whopper of a headache. She asked, "What happened?" as she pulled herself from the floor.

Agent Loso at the sensor board responded, "We are at a dead stop, Captain."

Smith reported, "All weapons and propulsion systems are off-line. The gravity generators are at half power. And the belly deck of the ship is entirely exposed to space. Fortunately, no one was down there."

"Begin organizing damage repair teams. Any vital technologies in the belly deck need to be re-shielded. We'll worry about restoring the deck when we get home."

"I'll get on it, Captain, but with only a skeleton crew onboard, it may take a while," Smith said.

"How much time has passed since we dropped out of LS?" Brooks questioned.

"One hour," Loso replied.

"An hour! That means that the Nazi arrived nearly forty five minutes ago."

"Unfortunately, that's correct, Captain. We dropped out of LS close enough to get some detailed scans. I am detecting a Nazi team aboard the *Rimcha*. I suspect they intend to salvage it for themselves," said Loso.

"That is one thing we can't let happen, but first I want to know what happened to us," said Brooks. Tilting her head toward the intercom in the ceiling, she asked, "Josh, are you still with us?"

"Yes, Captain – though I'm barely in one piece."

"What happened to the drive, Chief?"

Several decks below, sprawled in a maintenance tube near the tachyon drive, Austin wielded a tool adjusting a power junction as he reported, *"I haven't the slightest clue, Captain. Somehow all the tachyons have been drained from the drive. Once they were gone, the LS thrust destabilized, and we gradually slowed down. It's a good thing though; the core was reaching critical mass. If the tachyons hadn't been expelled, the ship would have ripped itself apart."*

"What happened to the tachyons?"

Austin did not reply to the Captain's question, but Loso did. "Captain, the *Rimcha* is emitting a strange energy field. It is like…" the B.O.T. swallowed hard, "…some sort of wake in space. It is flushing all the tachyon energy from our systems and dispersing it into space."

"Why?" Brooks asked.

Loso hypothesized, "Perhaps tachyon energy poses a threat to the alien vessel."

"Alien vessel – you're sure about that now?" Brooks asked.

"I believe there is now sufficient evidence to assume that the *Rimcha* is of extraterrestrial origin. Nothing we have observed about the vessel so far suggests that there is human technology involved. Further, aside from the Nazis, the scanners are detecting dozens of bodies aboard the *Rimcha*. They appear to be dead, and they are definitely not human."

Brooks gripped the back of her helm chair and braced herself against the surge of emotions building within her. This would be mankind's first encounter with an alien species. How she handled herself now would determine their survival if this vessel turned out to be a threat.

She ordered, "Bring the hydrogen thrusters online. They may not be the most efficient means of transportation available, but they're all we've got."

As Smith complied, Brooks turned to Loso, "Work with Chief Martinez. Try and find a way to use the Nazi TSJ to get aboard that Nazi vessel."

Loso asked, "Why, Captain?"

"There is a good chance that the Nazis have already equipped the alien vessel with a security force. I am betting they won't be too happy about receiving guests. However, if we can sneak aboard the Nazi vessel, we may be able to find a way to stop them before they complete their efforts on the *Rimcha*. We might also be able to obtain some power reserves for the station."

She turned to Smith and ordered, "Begin repairs, and start working on a scenario to board the alien ship. If the crew is dead, this is an invaluable opportunity to gain new technology and knowledge. And if we can find a way to contact the alien homeworld, we may just end up with a new ally in this war."

"What if they're hostile?" Smith asked.

"Only one way to find out. You have the bridge."

"And where will you be?"

"In the chapel."

"Now? It's not even 6:00 pm yet. Captain, we have more important things to worry about right now. I really must…"

"You have your orders, Commander. Carry on!" Brooks snapped, and she left the bridge.

~

On deck eight in the launch bay, Chief Klaus Martinez tinkered with his prized Nazi transport space jet. The vessel had performed superbly on its first mission and had fooled the Nazis completely. He was only sorry he had not been able to pilot her himself for her maiden voyage. However, now his tiny space jet was being rallied for yet another mission – perhaps of even greater importance than the original capture of the Space Port four years ago. He was excited beyond words, but still a little apprehensive about who his copilot would be.

Intelligence Agent Loso now stood in Martinez's launch bay, and he had just finished explaining the captain's orders for the two of them in his clipped mechanical voice. Not being human, Loso was extremely different from the rest of the crew, and very few besides the captain and Dr. Radcliff spent any real amount of time with him. Perhaps it was an unworthy prejudice, but there were those in Christian circles – even on the *Intruder* – who said the B.O.Ts. were an abomination. Over ambitious Nazi scientists had found a way to mutate reptilian DNA with human DNA and then clone and cybernetically enhance an artificial life form that had proved the ultimate weapon. Loso had been one of the original prototypes. This meant he had flaws and was eventually discarded by the Nazis. However, anything the Nazis thought of as useless usually ended up being very useful to the rebellion, and so Agent Loso had ultimately been folded into their ranks.

Martinez responded, "What did you have in mind?"

Loso continued his report, "The Nazi vessel in question is called the *Berserko*. According to our records, that vessel left the solar system the day we took control of the Space Port. It has not been heard from since until today, and given the four year communications blackout on the part of Nazis, we can assume that the crew of this vessel is unaware of our possession of the station. So we can..."

Martinez cut him off, "We can use some of the Nazi security codes we found on the Space Port to gain access to the vessel."

Loso grinned, revealing his razor-sharp, cybernetic teeth - a sight which slightly disturbed Martinez. Loso said, "That is my plan, Chief. Shall we proceed?"

"Let's get to work!" Martinez smiled back, with much smaller teeth admittedly, and gestured toward the Nazi TSJ.

~

On the bridge, Chief Austin manned the helm for Brooks. The *Intruder's* hydrogen thrusters were slowly bringing them closer to the alien ship. He reported, "We are moving at 11,000 kilometers per hour. By my estimates, we will reach the vessel in three hours. What is the status of the weapons?"

Smith tapped at her control board which stubbornly refused to operate correctly. She muttered a curse under her breath and then replied, "They are completely useless. All of our weapons are based on tachyon technology. If we can't find another way to defend ourselves, we have a snowball's chance in Hell of surviving."

"Relax, Commander. The captain has gotten us out of worse jams than this."

"The captain should be here now, doing her job! But instead she's down in the chapel wasting time." A few of the junior officers on the bridge cut Smith an exacerbated look, and she immediately regretted her words.

For Austin's part, he did not comment. It was no secret Smith was not a follower of Christ. There was no question she was brilliant. In addition to her expertise in weapons and linguistics, she also held degrees in mathematics, literature, and psychology. In her mid-thirties now, she had spent her twenties as a perpetual student. She had earned most of her degrees on Earth before the war, and then she had excelled in hand-to-hand combat training on Io. She was the perfect solider in every way, but somehow the idea of Christ just did not compute. Since it did for most of the rest of the crew, she tended to keep to herself.

Austin changed the subject, "We have several tons of explosive substances aboard, including nitroglycerin, methane, TNT, hydrogen, and a variety of others. Their effectiveness would be limited, but I believe we could use them to create a compliment of missiles."

Smith smiled and asked, "Is Doctor Radcliff onboard?"

Austin replied, "Yes, he is assisting the science team in analyzing the *Rimcha*. Why?"

"How many people are onboard?"

"Twenty, however, Loso and Martinez are preparing to head for the Nazi ship, you and I are at command posts, and the Captain is otherwise engaged. That leaves fifteen people."

"Have the doctor assemble a team of five, and have them begin construction of the weapons. Tell him to use his expertise to combine the chemicals to produce the most powerful missiles possible."

"You want the doctor to do that?"

Smith smirked and related, "Obviously, the doctor has never regaled you with the story of his year as a chemical engineer on the Mars colony. When the colony was under siege, he successfully combined a series of usually harmless chemicals to form a bomb. He left the bomb in the main entryway of his lab where he and about a dozen technicians had taken refuge. When the Nazis raided the lab, they were all killed instantly by the bomb, and Radcliff and his team escaped. I'm hoping the story isn't an exaggeration, but the doctor claims he can work wonders with chemicals."

"I'll get him started right away."

"I'll need a report from his team within one hour. Have the rest of the crew continue repairs."

"Aye, Commander!"

~

Aboard the Nazi vessel *Berserko*, a young officer's eyes narrowed at his display, and he called out to his commanding officer, "Captain Otomento, I am detecting a perimeter breech! Two vessels are approaching. One is a Confederation Transport Space Jet, and the other is the *R.S.S. Intruder*."

In his chair in the center of the *Berserko*'s bridge, the cynical B.O.T. captain moved a metal claw to his chin to ponder the report. Then he said, "Have the TSJ double back and attack the vessel. We have more important things to worry about."

The ensign argued, "But, sir, they don't stand a chance of stopping that vessel!"

Otomento calmly replied, "You underestimate our people, ensign."

Then the menacing B.O.T. rose, faced the young officer, and raising his arm, unleashed a violent surge of laser energy. The young ensign sizzled out of existence.

Otomento asked, "Would anyone else like to question my orders?"

There was a long pause, but finally the *Berserko's* first officer spoke up. "Of course not, sir. But begging the Captain's forgiveness, I do have news of merit."

Otomento nodded and the first officer, a Commander Zachary Morgan, reported, "For some reason, the jet is in black mode. They will not communicate with us. As for the *Intruder*, it poses no threat to us. The vessel is limping along at 11,000 kilometers per hour and has been heavily damaged. We will have our work on the alien craft completed long before they reach our position."

Otomento grimaced, but then said, "Keep an eye on it in any case, and have the crew of that jet report to me immediately upon their arrival."

~

"The heavens declare the glory of God;
  And the firmament shows His
    handiwork.
Day unto day utters speech
And night unto night reveals knowledge
There is no speech nor language
Where their voice is not heard
Their line has gone out through all the

Earth,
And their words to the end of the world…"

~

Captain Lori Brooks was again on her bridge, but the words of Psalm 19 refused to leave her mind. On the holographic viewer, the dead hulk of the *Rimcha* now spun silently in space with the shadow of the imposing *Berserko* draped across her. If Loso was right and a dead alien crew was aboard the *Rimcha*, that was something to be mourned, but she couldn't help but wonder in what ways God had *declared* Himself among them. As with the Scotty from the parallel universe, there was nothing that compelled her to believe there was more than one God in existence. So whoever these aliens were, their God would be the same as hers, and learning His story among them was something she was most eager to do.

She had brought this desire before the Lord, but not being her normal scheduled time, she had kept her prayer session brief. Still, something had compelled her to inquire of the Lord privately regardless. She knew as well as any that the privacy of the chapel was not required to communicate with God. For her though, being a captain was filled with a million distractions. If she didn't make the time to communicate with God privately, she likely never would, and that would be a huge loss. Not that Commander Smith felt that way. She and her tactical officer got along in every other area but this, and there had been an edge in Smith's voice from the moment her captain returned to the bridge.

Smith reported, "It would have been nice to have a little more help on this one, but I have figured out why our tachyons are being flushed away from the ship."

Brooks was well aware that the *little more help* she was referring to was supposed to be Brooks herself. The captain ignored the comment and instead asked, "And why is that?"

Austin came up to Smith's station and continued the report, "In their natural state, tachyons only travel slightly faster than light speed. The new LS drive speeds them up and uses them to create an energy bubble in space which then propels the ship. In the past, we have only been able to travel at about half light speed, because we haven't been able to properly maintain the energy bubble. The problem with the drive now that we can maintain the bubble is that the tachyon pressure field becomes too strong. So no matter how much we recalibrate the gravity generators, it won't stop the pressure from crushing the ship."

"That doesn't explain why the tachyons were drained from the ship?"

Smith continued, "According to our scans, the *Rimcha* also has an LS drive, but it's much more sophisticated. And it appears that their pressure field operates the opposite way that ours does. Instead of forcing the tachyon pressure inward toward the ship, the tachyons on the *Rimcha* force the fabric of space away from the ship. And since we know that objects that travel under the fabric of space (subspace if you will) travel much faster than those above the fabric, we can assume that the *Rimcha* can reach incredible speeds. So, somehow, when the tachyons from our engine touched the hull of that ship, it activated their pressure field. And since we were so far away at the time, their field expanded and flushed all of our tachyons away. But the field was too weak to propel us anywhere."

Brooks made a disappointed statement, "So the aliens use Black Vortex technology, just like the Nazis."

Though what Brooks had said was not really a question, Austin treated it like it was. He countered, "No, in fact, one could say that this technology could be classified as a *Blue Vortex*. It is far more stable and predictable than the Black Vortex. I don't think we could completely incorporate a matrix for the device into our systems without further detailed study, but if I could just get the schematics for one, I might be able to figure out a way to make our current LS drive more stable."

Brooks ordered, "Contact Loso, tell him he has a change of orders. He and Martinez are to find a way to get onboard the *Rimcha* and locate the matrix of the *Blue Vortex*. They are to take as many close range scans as they can. We'll take as many long range scans as we can to help them know what they're looking for. Once they complete their mission, I want them to find a way to destroy that alien ship. If we can't have it, I'm not about to let the Nazis have it."

Smith said, "I'll send a coded message at once, Captain."

Then Brooks said, "Get to work!" and she slid once more into her command chair.

Chapter 3
The *Berserko*

Loso stood before the captain of the *Berserko*, Otomento, a fellow B.O.T. However, there were very salient differences in their appearances. While Loso's DNA had been based on a handful of basic lizards, Otomento – clearly a newer model B.O.T. – was a mesh of several different species of reptile. Loso detected traces of alligator, iguana, and king cobra in the captain, and that was just for starters. There was no telling what other genetic secrets swam in this creature's blood. He hoped a cobra's ability to spit deadly venom was not part of Otomento's genetic makeup, but he wasn't going to take any chances. Not that venom would have been necessary. The laser canon that was integrated into his cybernetic arm looked more than deadly enough.

Otomento finally spoke, "State your identity."

Loso answered first, "I am B.O.T. Unit 3344.86, name, Namano, - rank, lieutenant."

Then Martinez, who stood beside him in a synthetic Nazi engineer's uniform, turned and faced Otomento. Captain Brooks had not told them anything like this was going to happen. He and Loso were simply supposed to sneak aboard the *Berserko* and do anything possible to derail the repair efforts on the *Rimcha*. Now, however, they had been forced to improvise.

Captain Brooks had ordered them to alter course and head for the *Rimcha* citing something about a new technology the captain was desperate to get scans of. However, only moments later, the *Berserko* had sent out an override code meant to command the TSJ to begin automated docking procedures. Technically speaking, a rebel TSJ would not have submitted to such an order, but had the Nazis suspected something was amiss, he and Loso would have been blown out of the stars.

Martinez spoke, "I am Chief Gregory Ball, supervising transport space jet construction attendant."

"What is your purpose in this region of space? Confederation Command seems to be under a communications blackout. All of our attempts to communicate with them have failed," said Otomento.

Loso knew exactly what to say, and at least for the moment, he could tell Otomento the truth. "We were sent here with some information. The rebels have captured the Space Port, and the Nazi command staff that was once stationed there has retreated to Earth. They have established a new command base in Paris, France."

Otomento could hardly believe his cybernetic ears, "Are you telling me that the rebels have seized control of the most powerful weapons in the solar system."

Martinez continued the report, "Yes, sir. Quite some time ago. We assumed by now the entire solar system would know."

"Not quite," said Otomento flatly, and then he pointed to the image of the *Rimcha* on the holographic viewer. He continued, "Four years ago, our vessel came under attack by a vessel very similar to this one. We used the Black Vortex to escape and ended up stranded in a desolate region of space light years away. Our damage was so extensive that we only recently made it back to Nazi controlled space. When we returned, we discovered this single vessel orbiting Pluto. We attacked them without mercy. We managed to breech their hull, and my tactical officer maneuvered three radiation charges inside. The ship tried to flee, but once the crew was dead, it fell adrift in space. My teams are working to vent the radiation now and to commandeer the ship. One can only imagine what secrets it holds!"

"Emperor Chu's thoughts exactly!" Martinez blurted out.

"His Majesty is aware of the *Rimcha*?" Otomento questioned.

Martinez swallowed hard and then said, "Yes, there is little that escapes his attention. The Confederation detected the alien vessel in orbit of Pluto weeks ago. As of yet, we have only been able to squeeze a few TSJs past the planetary force field. When the *Berserko* was detected in range, Emperor Chu sent us to convey the importance of getting it safely back to Earth. No doubt it has weapons we could use to help us reclaim or destroy the Space Port."

"We have been back in the solar system for less than two days. How could a TSJ have possibly made it all the way to Mars in that length of time?"

It was Loso's turn to add to the story. "You've been gone a long time. The planetary force field does not allow our ships to use the Black Vortex Matrix to escape the planet. However, our scientists have outfitted a fleet of TSJs with a miniature version of the technology. The range is not as extensive, but certainly far enough to reach the interior planets."

Martinez hoped his look of utter shock wasn't too obvious, and he immediately began praying the Nazis would not start dissecting his TSJ for the new technology. Needless to say, no TSJ he had ever heard of was equipped with Black Vortex technology.

Loso held out an electronic pad and said, "You are hereby ordered to grant us unrestricted access to the alien vessel. Chu wants the specifications for their weapons, propulsion, and any other major technologies transmitted to him immediately."

Otomento glanced at the pad and a scrolling list of codes. He said, "We have not been privy to the latest encryption codes for almost four years. We cannot decode this."

"That's all right, Captain. Your reputation is a strong one with the emperor. We will provide you with an update package as soon as possible. In the meantime, our orders cannot wait."

It was a huge bluff, and Martinez did not believe for an instant that Otomento would fall for it. Surprisingly though, he did.

"Very well. Take your jet over. I will inform my boarding party."

Loso nodded at the captain in acknowledgement, and almost simultaneously a cybernetic indicator began to flash on the back of his neck. He was receiving a transmission only he could hear, and it said, *"Loso, this is Captain Brooks. I am transmitting our final long range scans to you now. The Rimcha's primary LS drive is located near the heart of the vessel. There appear to be five power cells attached to it. The energy signatures seem to be compatible with the station. Take detailed scans of the drive and then remove the cells. They appear to be fairly small, but they hold enough energy to power the station for another three years. You should also locate the weapons manifold. If you can trigger an overload in the manifold, it will destroy the vessel. Proceed with caution, but also with haste. Brooks out!"*

Despite the fact that no one else could hear the message, Otomento was the first to notice the flashing indicator on Loso's neck. He said, "You just received a transmission. What did it say?"

Loso knew he had to be careful. If the story he was about to tell Otomento was not convincing, Otomento would most likely have he and Martinez detained or at worst executed immediately. He said with conviction, "It was a transmission from Command. HQ wants you to keep close tabs on the *Intruder*. They may be temporarily incapacitated, but they are in no worse condition than they were when they destroyed the SYCO."

Otomento flared, "What? You're telling me the SYCO is gone! Were there any survivors?" He had good reason to be concerned. He and the captain of the SYCO, a fellow B.O.T., had been created in the same laboratory and thus were very close.

Loso said flatly, "No." Then he continued his report. "Command also wishes us to proceed with our mission immediately, or even more lives could be lost at the hands of the rebels."

Martinez had never been good at trying to read the emotions on a B.O.T's face. But he was not surprised when Otomento raged, "And while you do that, I'll blow the *Intruder* straight to Hell!"

Loso grimaced and quickly countered, "Emperor Chu does not want you to do that! He has other, more appropriate plans for the *Intruder*."

Otomento was too angry to even ask what those plans were. Loso was glad for this. He was getting a little tired of making things up as he went along. He turned once more toward Otomento and said, "If you will excuse us, sir."

Otomento nodded, and they turned and headed toward the exit, but just as they thought they were home free, Otomento said, "Lt. Namano, for your sake, I hope you have been telling me the truth. If not, the consequences would be rather unpleasant. My men will be watching you."

Loso nodded at this, but Martinez's body began to drip with sweat. He didn't even want to imagine what kind of torments a B.O.T. like Otomento was capable of inflicting.

~

"We've had to drop another 1,000 kilometers per hour, Captain. At the rate we're going through our hydrogen supply, I don't think we'll ever reach the *Rimcha*," reported Chief Engineer Josh Austin.

"How much farther do we have to go?" Brooks questioned.

"Still about 21,000 kilometers, Captain, but we'll run out of fuel before we make another 10,000. We have a full complement of TSJs. Perhaps we should send them ahead," Austin suggested.

"No, they'd be too vulnerable. Besides, can't our inertia carry us for a while to help save fuel?" Brooks asked.

"Ordinarily, yes, but the same tachyon repulsion field is creating some sort of spatial drag. It's killing our inertia."

Brooks nodded and said, "I appreciate your efforts, Josh, but I think you should turn your attention back to getting the LS drive online. Even if you can get the old sub-LS thrusters recharged that will at least be something."

"I'll try, Captain, but honestly, without tachyons, I don't see how we can possibly recharge the engines."

"Perhaps we've been going about this the wrong way. We've been trying to get closer to the *Rimcha*; maybe we should use our last bit of fuel to try and move out of range of the tachyon expulsion field," Smith suggested.

"It's too late for that, even if we could theoretically get beyond the field," Austin dismissed.

"Then I guess the most we can all do is pray for the success of Loso and Martinez. It looks like they are our only hope at the moment," Brooks said, trying to keep doubt from her voice.

Smith tried to raise the spirits of her fellow officers, which was extremely out of the ordinary for her. "Look on the bright side, the doctor has our new weapons online."

Brooks smiled at that. Not that it would make much difference, but she asked anyway, "What can we expect from them?"

Smith relayed, "Thanks to the doctor, we should be able to punch a hole or two through the *Berserko's* hull.

But we'll have to fire the missiles from pointblank range. We'd have to get within at least forty feet of their hull."

Brooks bared her teeth in disgust at that notion. At optimal strength, the *Intruder's* weapons had a maximum range of one light second, or about 186,000 miles. The rebels tended to want to keep as much distance as possible between themselves and an often superior Nazi vessel. Having to fly within forty feet would be literal suicide. It was fortunate, in a twisted sort of way, that the *Intruder's* current fuel crisis would prevent them from having to test the new weapons out, or so Brooks thought for the briefest of all possible moments.

Smith shouted, "Captain, the *Berserko* is on an interception course. They'll be here in less than two minutes!"

Brooks sprinted to the helm and ordered, "All hands report to battle stations! Chief Austin, get down to the environmental controls."

Austin was puzzled, but Brooks quickly explained, "If you can adjust the airlocks, we may be able to convert them into crude thrusters."

"You mean explosive decompression thrusters?"

"That's right! It should give us an extra edge in maneuvering, even with our hydrogen thrusters impaired."

Austin nodded and was gone without another word. Brooks turned back to her board and smirked. *Lt. Fields was not going to be happy about missing this.*

~

Loso turned to his Nazi escort and bellowed, "Captain Otomento is disobeying a direct order. I told him to leave the *Intruder* alone!"

As he said this, he adjusted his portable scanner. He and his Nazi escort were standing directly in front of the *Rimcha's* LS drive. Unlike the *Intruder*, the core of the drive was not contained inside a tiny cubicle. Rather, it rested at the heart of a massive engineering bay with thousands of alien control panels and thousands of flickering, colored lights. The core itself resembled a rectangular glass box. Through the alien glass, Loso could see tachyon energy particles swirling in an emerald rainbow of color, but he found it remarkable that the dominant color of the bay, and the whole ship for that matter, was purple.

The young Nazi didn't even flinch at Loso's complaint. He said, "The captain does not take orders from a mere lieutenant. Besides, I have been informed he intends to capture the vessel, not destroy it. How did you find out about the attack in any case?"

"Have you forgotten I am in constant contact with Command? They are monitoring the situation."

"Why not send those messages to the *Berserko* directly?"

"Your captain himself said your codes were out of date, and you have been out of communication for years. Emperor Chu is not about to trust your crew with classified data until you have been debriefed."

That seemed to content the young ensign, and at that instant, the B.O.T.'s scanner began to chime. He directed his gaze toward the scanner's tiny screen and had to choke back his shout of excitement. The device had completed its scan of the entire LS drive. The energy cells would be compatible with the station and would provide them with energy for years to come. Further, the design of the Blue Vortex was not altogether beyond human comprehension or the resources of the rebels. In time, he had no doubt they would master it.

Loso ordered, "Get some men in here and have them disconnect those energy cells. Then take them to my TSJ."

"Why?" the ensign asked.

"The Emperor wants samples of the alien technology." Then there was a click in Loso's mechanical arm and his built in laser whirled into life. Granted, his laser was actually just a welding tool - nothing compared to the one Otomento had installed - but the ensign seemed to get the point.

"I'll get on it right away, sir."

Loso nodded and grinned as the ensign began summoning his fellows. He hoped the *Intruder* would be able to evade the *Berserko*, but Captain Brooks had been through worse. The real question was, could Martinez finish his task of rigging the *Rimcha* to self-destruct, and could they get out of here alive and with their new technologies? Those were questions that he had far too many doubts had an answer of *yes*.

Chapter 4
The *Rimcha*

"You know, Scotty, you've yet to mention what these aliens look like, or even what they're called," Gloria Moonbeam pointed out.

Up until now, the only light in the library had been provided from the afternoon sun through a large, westward-facing bay window. Now, the light of the setting sun had turned the room decidedly orange. Scotty lit a candle in the center of his table and leaned forward as if he was about to relay highly sensitive information.

"What they're called is a story for another day, I think. Even the rebels and Nazis won't learn that for now. As for what they look like, I'm thinking of something like the classic little green men."

"Oh, come on; that's so cliché! You can think of something better."

"I suppose you think I should make them bears?"

"You could do worse," Gloria snickered.

Scotty shook his head in protest and said, "No, it's the classic little aliens or nothing."

"All right, you win. Now, what happens next?"

"Well…"

~

"For the last time, would you stop looking over my shoulder?" Martinez raged.

He had been given a very annoying and very young Nazi escort. Though Martinez did not support anything the Nazis did, he could not understand why they had let this young officer assimilate into their ranks. The Nazis were interested in producing a master race of humans, but this young man was scrawny and quite nerdy. Martinez could only assume they kept him around to plant a thorn in the sides of people like he and Loso.

"I am sorry, Chief, but the Captain told me to keep an eye on you."

"He said to keep an eye on *me* - not my work! These scans are classified. Only Lt. Lo…Namano and I are allowed to review them."

The Nazi's eyes went cold, and he asked, "What did you say?"

"What?"

"It sounded like you started to say, Loso – Loso the traitor of the B.O.Ts. His intelligence file was in the last classified package we received before we left the solar system. I remember reading it. He was reprogrammed by the rebels and infiltrated several Nazi bases, but he slipped up and used one of his old access codes from before he was *converted*. That was the first clue that he was still alive. Since that time, everyone has been on the watch for him, but you should know that if you are who you say you are."

Martinez did not even meet the ensign's gaze. Instead, he continued to focus on his scans as he retorted, "I do, and you are wasting my time. Lt. Namano would be insulted to be compared to that traitor!"

Ensign Nerdy nodded and then asked, "What did you say your name was again, Chief?"

"What?"

"Your name. It's a simple enough question."

Martinez opened his mouth and then suddenly stuttered. He had never considered himself spy-worthy, and this moment was proving the point. He had drawn a complete blank.

"It was – is – Chief…."

"Wasn't it Chief Balk?"

"Yes, yes, that's it! Chief Balk!"

The young Nazi withdrew his sidearm and directed it toward Martinez. "The name was Ball, Chief Gregory Ball."

Martinez looked up and stared into the barrel of the laser pistol pointed directly at him, certain his life was about to end. He had known something like this was going to happen! For being such a wimp, this Nazi was no idiot. Martinez's only hope lay in a very classic joke; one he could hardly expect the Nazi to fall for, but he had to try. He raised his arm and pointed beyond the officer. Then he shouted, "What the heck is that?"

The Nazi hesitated a second, but finally could not resist looking. When he did, Martinez bolted. He dashed down disorganized corridors, vaulting over alien corpses still littering the deck in the process. If he managed to survive this, he'd have a report sure to thrill Dr. Radcliff, but his survival was certainly a big *if* at the moment. He stumbled to the deck, and hearing the footfalls of the Nazi in hot pursuit, he leapt into an access tube, cracking a rib as he collided with the metal edge of the port. The weapons manifold was only a few meters away. Unfortunately, he feared a deadly confrontation would take place before he reached it.

~

Brooks stilled herself once more against the sudden impact of a Nazi weapons blast. So far, the *Intruder's* new titanium armor was holding its own against the attack, but Brooks knew it would not be long before the Nazis broke through their defenses.

At tactical, Lt. Commander Smith shouted, "I've launched another round of missiles, but other than a few scrapes, they aren't causing much damage to the Nazi ship. We need to get closer!"

Brooks at the helm, who was already spinning the *Intruder* about like a ballerina trying to avoid the Nazi fire, said, "We can't risk letting them have a clear shot. If we get shot down, Loso and Martinez don't stand a chance. We'll just have to keep the Nazis distracted until they get back."

"Then we'd better be ready to run like Hell once they do!" Smith cursed as she unleashed yet another round of chemical missiles.

Brooks turned to her and with uncharacteristic sarcasm said, "Preparing to initiate the *Run like Hell Maneuver.*"

Smith only chuckled at that, but Brooks spoke again before the Commander could form a rebuttal, "I'm receiving a transmission...It's from Loso! He has the data and the energy cells. He is making his way back to the TSJ."

Smith asked, "That's good news, but what about Martinez?"

"No word."

Anguish and anger did a macabre dance across Smith's face before she had a chance to repress them. Martinez was a close friend, but her duties and the present crisis demanded that she keep her cool. Instead of freaking out, she reported, "Captain, even if we do get them both back safely, I'm not sure we'll be able to get away from the *Berserko*. It is likely they'll destroy us before we can get too far from the *Rimcha*."

Brooks was not even worried. "I don't think that is going to happen, Commander. Have you noticed that only one out of every three shots has hit the *Intruder*? I'm a good pilot, but I can't believe the Nazis are that bad when it comes to targeting. And have you also noticed how none of their shots has damaged any critical system? I'd say it's more likely that they plan to capture our ship. But you're right; we'll need a plan on how to get out of here."

Smith had no idea how to accomplish that, but Austin, who had been listening over the intercom, suggested, *"Captain what about the Nazi TSJ?"*

Brooks did not realize he was making a suggestion and said, "They'll need to steer clear of the battle."

"No, Captain, I meant, can't we use it to our advantage? After all, as far we know, the Nazis still think it is their ship. Have Loso and Martinez return and dock with the Berserko momentarily. The jet has a compliment of twenty micro-missiles. If Loso puts a few in the Berserko's airlock and sets them to detonate on a delay, it…"

"It will rip open the belly of their hull' Good thinking, Chief. It could work, Captain!" Smith sounded.

"Very well, I'll send a coded message to Loso. Hopefully the *Berserko* is still in the jet's range."

"Just barely, Captain. I suggest we bridge the gap a little," Austin suggested.

"I guess there goes the rest of our fuel," Brooks quipped.

~

Aboard the *Berserko*, Otomento smirked, "Their vessel is proving less of a threat than Lt. Namano reported." Then he asked, "What is the status of our repair team on the *Rimcha?*"

A young ensign answered him, "I'm receiving a report of a disturbance aboard the alien vessel." Then for some reason the ensign halted his report, and his eyes grew wide with terror!

Otomento barked, "What is it?" But his answer did not come from the ensign. In a flash of fire and flesh searing radiation, the bridge of the *Berserko* began to glow. Otomento saw his crew melt into puddles of gooey blood and flesh before his eyes. Screams of agony cascaded through his cybernetic ears, even as his own reptilian flesh began to crisp. With great effort and pain, he staggered from the bridge.

Two soldiers rushed to him as he stumbled to the deck in the corridor. "What happened?" the B.O.T. captain demanded.

"We're not sure, Captain. Radiation is flooding the upper decks. We need to get to the auxiliary command deck below before…" but it was too late. Otomento saw those men melt into puddles of goo as well. For the moment, his cybernetic structure was preserving his life, but he was still in agony. He stood and stumbled into the nearest lift. He barely had time to direct it toward auxiliary control before everything around him faded to black.

~

"Captain, are you seeing this?" Smith bellowed.

"Yes…yes! It looks like we won't have to send the TSJ back there after all."

"What is going on?" Austin sounded over the comm.

"The *Rimcha* just enveloped the upper decks of the *Berserko* in a radiation beam. They have broken off their attack," Brooks reported.

"I thought the crew on that ship was dead."

"Those are still my readings, Captain," Smith confirmed.

"If I had to guess, I'd say Loso and Martinez had something to do with this."

~

"Wow! Well, I hope that helps," Chief Klaus Martinez said with half a laugh. He had finally managed to lose Ensign Nerdy Nazi and had made it to the weapons control room of the *Rimcha*. Though complex, the alien displays had allowed him to monitor the battle. The *Intruder* appeared to be holding its own, but that would likely not last long. In almost mock frustration, he had pounded his fist on the image of the *Berserko* on the screen, and instantaneously a purple beam had enveloped the *Berserko*. After that, the ship just hung lifeless in space. He just hoped the rest of the weapons systems were as user friendly.

Ten minutes passed, and he completed his scans of the weaponry core, with still no sign of his Nazi pursuer. *Odd, this would have been the first place he would have looked had the situation been reversed.* Loso would be waiting by now at the TSJ. There was just one last thing to do.

The controls of the weapons power core consisted of a series of tubes and switches with a two dimensional purple keypad that operated the unit. According to the *Intruder's* initial scans, flipping each switch to the opposite direction of its current position would trigger an overload. However, the task was not as easy as it sounded. For not only did Martinez have to fiddle around with the key pad to unlock each switch from its position, but the endless series of alien tubes was also proving to be a distraction. Every tube was black with a slightly purple gloss over the top, and each tube seemed to breathe as if it were a living organism. A fact which Martinez could not discount given that to the touch the tubes felt organic.

Finally, however, he completed his task.

"Lt. Namano to Chief Ball, what's the hold up?" sounded Loso's voice over Martinez's private communicator.

"Sorry, sir. I'm almost done here. Is the jet ready for launch?"

"For quite a while now."

"Good, give me three more minutes, and I'll be there. If I'm not, leave without me, because I'll likely be dead."

"Three minutes, Chief!"

Martinez balked a bit that Loso had not tried to protest the arbitrary countdown to his doom. The B.O.T. was nothing if not practical.

The chief shook off any hurt feelings and set back to his work. All that remained was to flip one final switch - one which was far larger than the others. It was over half a meter wide and at least a meter in length. To make matters worse, at least six of the alien tubes slithered across it like snakes, and Martinez detested snakes.

Taking a deep breath, he headed toward the switch, but he barely got half a step before the panel beside him exploded in a wash of rainbow light. Martinez whirled to see the enflamed eyes of his annoying Nazi escort, but the man had changed. No longer did his body look meek and nerdy. Now his back was stiffened, and he towered over Martinez by several inches. His face was cold and his expression was like that of a cobra who was just about ready to make a kill. This was obvious by the huge Nazi laser rifle he now wielded.

For a moment, Martinez stood still, and the Nazi moved forward. It was not until Martinez could smell the odor of the man's sweat drenched body that he made any move. Lashing out, he grabbed the man by the wrist and shook his weapon loose. It fell away down the corridor. As Martinez lunged after it, the Nazi sunk his fingers painfully into Martinez's shoulder. Then he spun the Chief around and hammered his fist straight into Martinez's jaw. Tasting a mixture of blood and sweat, Martinez crashed to the deck, which was not necessarily a bad thing, because he fell into the exact position needed to knock the Nazi from his feet.

Like lightning, his legs darted forward catching the Nazi in the knee. Within seconds the man was on the floor alongside him, but Martinez sprang to his feet and picked up the orphaned rifle. Before the Nazi could react, Martinez unleashed a blast that vaporized him instantly. Then setting the weapon down, he went back to his work. All this had cost him a solid minute.

~

"Nothing like keeping 10 seconds for wiggle room!" Loso mocked as Martinez jumped into the cockpit of the TSJ.

"Sorry, sir; I ran into a delay. And we're not out of the woods yet. The weapons core is overloading. We have to clear 20,000 kilometers within the next 60 seconds, or we'll be destroyed along with the *Rimcha*."

"Can this ship go that fast?"

"Not really!"

"Great!"

"Hang on, sir. This is bound to get a little bumpy."

~

Smith reported, "The TSJ is launching. Loso reports the weapons manifold will overload in less than one minute."

Brooks asked, "Will they clear the blast radius?"

"Barely, Captain…if they're lucky."

It's a good thing I believe in a little more than luck, Brooks said to herself. Then she asked, "What's the status of the *Berserko*?"

"I don't think they'll pose much of a threat. Her bridge and main viewing sphere have been destroyed. They still have power and control on the lower decks, but it looks like they have yet to rally themselves back into fighting form. It will take several weeks' worth of repairs before she is going to be a serious threat to anyone again."

"That's certainly good news!" smiled Brooks. Then she reported, "We're down to 20 seconds. What's the status of the TSJ?"

"I've never seen one move that fast, but it's not going to be enough to clear the blast radius."

Brooks and Smith watched the holoviewer for what they assumed would be the final seconds of their friends' lives. Finally Smith began to countdown, "10…9…8…7…6…5…4…3…2…1."

With the termination of the countdown, they both waited for the inevitable explosion, but it never came. On the screen, the image of the *Rimcha* still spun in space quietly, but something about the ship had changed. In a moment, the curious observations of Brooks, Smith, and likely several others on the crew turned to utter terror. Where the ship had once been a perfect saucer, it now had a section that was clearly missing. An entire side of the vessel looked like it had been bitten like a doughnut. It was no longer curved, but completely straight. Brooks and Smith searched the screen for the missing section, and it didn't take long to locate. It was spiraling away from the vessel into a decaying orbit around Mars. After only a moment longer, the prodigal compartment blew apart in a surge of radiation that washed against the *Rimcha* with little more effect than a gentle wave.

Smith reported somberly, "The weapons manifold has been destroyed. The alien vessel is powering up, and they are locking some sort of towing beam onto the *Berserko*. The two vessels are moving away."

"The TSJ?" Brooks questioned, trying to choke back a few frustrated tears.

"They made it, Captain. They're fine. Loso reports they have the schematics requested and the energy cells."

"At least something good came out of all this. I'm setting a course to rendezvous with the jet. Once the LS core is back online, we'll head home with all speed. Something tells me this won't be the last time we'll see the *Berserko*...or the *Rimcha*."

After

"That's the way I see things happening, anyway," said Scotty Fields as he folded his hands on the table in front of him.

Gloria Moonbeam smirked, "You know, I think you missed your calling. You'd make a good author."

"Nah, the whole interplanetary emperor gig keeps me pretty busy."

"So what's next for the rebels? Will they ever face the *Berserko* or the *Rimcha* again?"

"I wouldn't be surprised, but that is a story for another day. Come on, Gloria. Let's go get some dinner!"

~

The Adventure continues in Book 3…
Parallel Encounters
Allegiance

Other exciting titles from *Thrive Christian Press* include:
Chronicles of the Imagination: Staranana
ISBN 978-0-9800600-1-0

After enduring centuries under a vicious tyrant, the people of the icy planet Staranana must decide whether to abandon their faith or continue to trust in the promises of God. The results of that decision will spark an adventure beyond the imagination!

Chronicles of the Imagination: Lizard Face
ISBN 978-0-9800600-3-4

A time of peace has dawned, but on the eve of the first Christmas on Staranana, an ancient enemy returns. Faith, friendship, and family will all be tested, and a single wrong decision could very well spell the doom of Staranana!

Chronicles of the Imagination: Nana-Old Testament
ISBN 978-0-9800600-6-5

The Starananians find themselves stranded in Earth's biblical past, and if they are to find their way home, they'll have to enlist the help of some of the greatest characters from throughout the *Old Testament*.

Chronicles of the Imagination: Nana-New Testament
ISBN 978-0-9800600-7-2

Having been trapped in the biblical past for months, hope is fading from the hearts of the Starananians. If they are to make it home, they must seek out the source of hope Himself, but this adventure won't end until the blood of one of them has been shed.

Find them today at www.amazon.com in paperback as well as on *Amazon Kindle* and *Barnes & Noble Nook*.

Check out these other *Classroom Classics* from *Thrive Christian Press*:

Rudyard Kipling's The *Jungle Book* – *Enhanced Classroom Edition*
ISBN – 978-0-615-70585-9

From Mowgli's relentless battle against the man-eating tiger Shere Khan to Rikki-Tikki-Tavi's great war against the sinister cobras Nag and Nagaina, Rudyard Kipling's classic *The Jungle Book* has been filling our lives with excitement for more than a century now. No personal library is complete without this timeless novel, and this edition enhanced for use in the classroom is a must have for any teacher about to embark on this literary adventure.

Steven Crane's *The Red Badge of Courage: Enhanced Classroom Edition*
ISBN – 978-0-615-80812-3

How does a coward become a hero? Henry Fleming is about to face that very question. Though he had, "...dreamed of battles all his life...", he soon finds that a soldier's life is more than he bargained for, and a single wrong decision runs the risk of branding him a coward for what little of his life he thinks he has left. Will he ultimately find the hero within, earning, if necessary, his own red badge of courage, or will he die a coward?

Sir Arthur Conan Doyle's *The Hound of the Baskervilles –*
Enhanced Classroom Edition
ISBN – 978-0-615-83170-1

There is a realm in which the most experienced of detectives is helpless – The Supernatural, and master detective Sherlock Holmes is about to plunge headfirst into that realm in this stunning adventure. *The Hound of the Baskervilles* takes Holmes and Dr. Watson to the Baskerville Estate where a mysterious hound of Hell has caused the deaths of many members of the Baskerville family. Will Holmes be able to crack this case before the latest heir to the Baskerville fortune meets his demise?

Also available…

To Kill a King
by Anna and Claire Trujillo
ISBN 978-0-9800600-8-9

Linna, a fighter in training in the futuristic city-state of Domina, has been marked for death by her own father. Her only hope of survival is to assassinate an enemy king, but is she brutal enough to carry out the deed?

Green Elephant – A "You Can Write" Activity Book
ISBN 978-1-4776-2830-0

Is there a great writer in you? *Green Elephant – A "You Can Write" Activity Book* uses a story written by a child to teach children how to write stories. The activity book also includes space for young authors to write their own stories and draw their own illustrations.

Thrive Christian Press is eager to see the Gospel of Jesus Christ spread throughout the world. If you would like 70% of the royalties from your most recent purchase donated to a Christian missionary or ministry of your choice, please complete the form below and mail to:

Missionary Donation Request
Thrive Christian Press
1120 Huffman Rd. Ste. 24-447
Anchorage, AK 99515

Missionary Name _____

Christian Ministry _____

Ministry Address _____

_____

Ministry Website _____

              Can we donate via this site?   *Yes*   *No*

Ministry Email _____

Title Purchased _____

Retailer Amazon.com   CreateSpace.com   Barnesandnoble.com

Please include a copy of your receipt. Visit www.thrivechristianpress.com to submit your request via email. Click on the *Mission Support* tab.

*All donations are subject to verification of the Christian ministry in question and purchase. Not all Thrive Christian Press titles qualify. Donations will be made in electronic form on ministry websites. Payment will be made within 60 days of request. This form is for paperback titles only. Please visit www.thrivechristianpress.com to request a donation for a Nook or Kindle title.

Donations by Title & Retailer

The Betrayal of Kelcott

Amazon	CreateSpace	B&N	Kindle	Nook
$1.00	$1.85	$0.17	$1.46	$1.36

Chronicles of the Imagination: Staranana

Amazon	CreateSpace	B&N	Kindle	Nook
$1.47	$3.16	N/A	$1.95	$1.81

Chronicles of the Imagination: Lizard Face

Amazon	CreateSpace	B&N	Kindle	Nook
$1.37	$3.05	N/A	$1.95	$1.81

Chronicles of the Imagination: Nana-Old Testament

Amazon	CreateSpace	B&N	Kindle	Nook
$0.83	$2.93	N/A	$2.44	$2.27

Chronicles of the Imagination: Nana-New Testament

Amazon	CreateSpace	B&N	Kindle	Nook
$1.00	$3.00	N/A	$2.44	$2.27

Green Elephant

Amazon	CreateSpace	B&N	Kindle	Nook
$1.67	$3.00	$0.24	N/A	N/A

The Hound of the Baskervilles

Amazon	CreateSpace	B&N	Kindle	Nook
$1.50	$2.90	$0.09	$1.96	$1.68

Parallel Encounters

Amazon	CreateSpace	B&N	Kindle	Nook
$1.00	$1.85	$0.17	N/A	N/A

All donation amounts are subject to change at any time and without notice. Donations are made to legitimate Christian organizations only, and all such organizations should be in close agreement with the Thrive Christian Press statement of faith. Requests for donations to organizations that do not meet these criteria will be declined. Purchase required to donate, but purchase does not guarantee donation. See www.thrivechristianpress.com for more details.